A catalogue record for this book is available from the British Library

Published by Ladybird Books Ltd
80 Strand, London, WC2R 0RL
A Penguin Company

ISBN: 978-184646-929-9

Printed in China

Alfie Kitten
Makes a Friend

written by Joan Stimson
illustrated by Simona Dimitri

Alfie Kitten was the cheekiest cat in the entire neighbourhood. He thought up the most brilliant games. He never ran out of jokes. And, when Alfie was around, it was almost impossible not to smile.

6

One day a new tabby kitten came to the neighbourhood. She was snooty and sniffy. She was vain and a pain. And right from the start she made it clear she was too busy worrying about her looks to enjoy herself.

"Don't take any notice," said Alfie's friends.

But Alfie couldn't bear to think of anyone not having fun. So the next day he bounded up to the new kitten with a cheerful, "Tabby Scowler, come and play. Try a smile and make my day!"

And then he began to tell his cheekiest puppy joke.

Alfie's friends laughed so loudly that
he could hardly hear himself speak.
Tabby thought the joke was funny too.

But then she remembered: "I've just
arranged my whiskers. if I have a good
laugh, they'll get in a tangle again."

So, instead of joining in, Tabby simply scowled some more. And stuck her nose in the air.

RINGSEND BRANCH TEL. 6680063

11

Alfie was disappointed. But the next day he bounded up to the new kitten with a cheerful, "Tabby Scowler, come and play. Try a smile and make my day!"

And then he began to describe his latest game. "It's called Run, Wriggle and Roll," said Alfie.

His friends were already purring expectantly. But Tabby looked confused. So Alfie explained. "Run around the garden, wriggle through the hedge and roll down the bank."

Whoooosh! The other kittens all rushed off together.

For a moment Tabby was caught up in the excitement too. But, as the other kittens disappeared into the hedge, she remembered: "I've just washed my fur. And, if I wriggle and roll, it will get all messy again."

So, instead of joining in, Tabby simply scowled some more. And stuck her nose in the air.

Alfie was shocked. But that evening he bounded up to the new kitten with a cheerful, "Tabby Scowler, come and play. Try a smile and make my day!"

And then he began to set up his moonlight shadow show. His friends were already practising bending and twisting by the wall.

Tabby thought perhaps she could make an exciting shadow shape too. But then she remembered: "I've just draped myself elegantly over the wall. And, if I twist my tail into a snake, I might not be able to make it elegant again."

So, instead of joining in, Tabby simply scowled some more. And stuck her nose in the air.

Alfie was beside himself.

"Don't give her a second thought," said all his friends. But Alfie was determined.

"I'll make that kitten enjoy herself," he announced, "if it's the last thing I do."

The next day Alfie waited patiently for his chance. And that afternoon he crept up to the new kitten… in total silence. The sun was warm. And Tabby was taking a cat nap.

"If I can just find her tickle spot," thought Alfie to himself, "then she's bound to burst out…"

"How *dare* you disturb my beauty sleep!" roared Tabby. And suddenly she was wide awake and furious!

Tabby chased Alfie right round the garden. She leapt after him as he dived for the safety of the hedge. And, when Alfie rolled head over paws down the bank, Tabby somersaulted after him.

23

By the time she caught up with Alfie,
Tabby was a changed kitten.

"He's gone too far this time," groaned all
Alfie's friends.

"Shall I help you re-arrange your whiskers?"
asked Alfie.

24

"No!" bellowed Tabby. "I'm enjoying myself far too much to worry about my whiskers," she explained. "And after that amazing chase, I'm in the mood for a good joke!"

"Now," she nudged Alfie. "Have you heard the one about the puppy from Peru?"

Alfie shook his head in astonishment.

"Well," went on the new kitten,
"There once was a puppy I knew,
Who lived on the plains of Peru.
He wasn't too bright,
But he danced every night
As he dined upon dinosaur stew!"

Then she rolled around the grass in hysterics.

It made Alfie's day to see Tabby enjoying herself.

And, from then on, whenever he thought up a new game, Alfie could be sure that Tabby Smiler would be the first to join in!

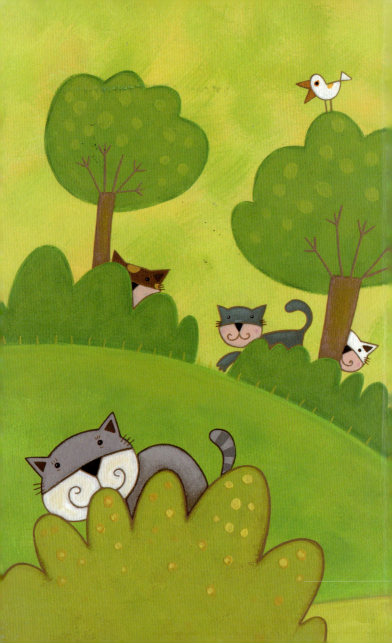